THE BOOK
NOBODY
WANTED TO READ
...BESIDES
YOU!

WRITTEN BY
IVON HICKMON

ILLUSTRARTED BY
BRANDON VAN LEER

DEDICATION

To my Wife and the other women most dearest to my heart, Thank You. Thank you for supporting, encouraging, and loving all of me. To my Daughters (Joydan and Ivy), Goddaughter, nieces, nephews, and little cousins: Always dream and always believe in yourself just enough to become IT. I am grateful for my brothers who pushed me along this journey. Most of all, to my Dad. Your co-sign was all that I needed. I know you are proud and celebrating with me.

- Ivon Hickmon

Cover and illustrations designed by Brandon Van Leer.

"Always do your best in whatever you do, never give less than 100% ! "

- Brandon Van Leer

To see more of Brandon's work, please visit vanleerart.com

Books may be purchased in quantity and/or special sales by contacting the author.

Visit www.TheHickmonHelper.com for details and more about the author.

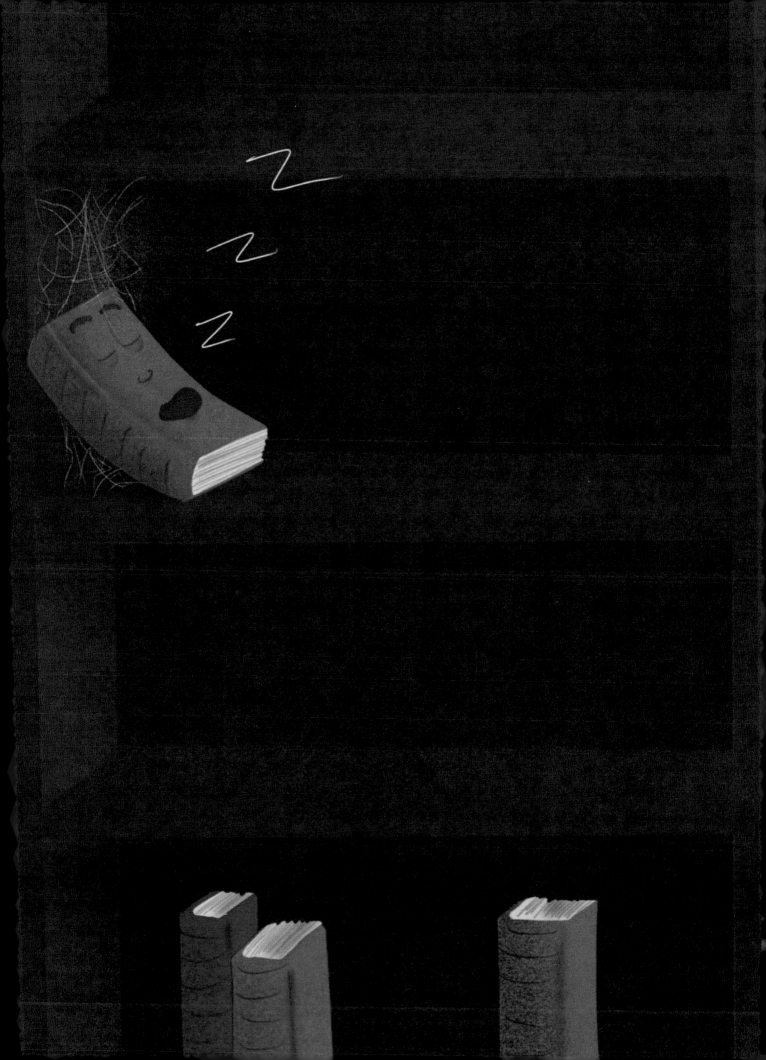

"I'll start by saying thank you for picking me up.
My name is Book and you must be . . . Reader?
It's so nice to meet you!" said Book.

"Are you going to say anything?

You know, most of the time when a person says "thank you" they usually get a response.

You're not saying anything! What kind of reader are you? A simple "Your welcome . . . not a problem . . . anytime" would do!

Where are your manners Reader?" cried Book.

I can only imagine . . .

Pause . . .

okay, so I need you . . .

YES YOU!

I need you to use your

imagination with me – ok?

(clears throat) Emm. Umm hmmm.

I can only imagine . . .

Riinnngggg . . . Riinnngggg . . . Riinnngggg . . .
"Pizza Palace, how may I help you?"

The hungry caller replies,
"Yes, can I order 3 large pepperoni pizzas?
Make one with extra anchovies.
I mean extra, extra, extra anchovies please!

Oh and by the way, can you throw in that
Book Nobody Wanted to Read. . . Besides You?

I just **love** that book!"

Ahhh. The thought of a reader wanting to read me, ahhh . . .
That gives me goosebumps just thinking about it!

Someone who thinks I am special enough to
be carried around everywhere they go.

I've had enough of this! I can see why nobody wants to read you! Since I've picked you up, you have done nothing but complain complain and complain!

Now you listen up, I have to tell you something with utmost importance.

Are you listening Book?

You are truly special.

I have an idea;
let's ask a couple of your
friends what they think
about you.

"Mr. Dust,
why do you like Book?"
Reader asked Mr. Dust.

"Well Book, many days and nights, you allowed me to sleep on you. You never say a mean word to me and you are always there for me.

Thank you for being a good friend" replied Mr. Dust.

Reader turns and asked,
"Miss Bookmark, do have anything to add?"

Smiling, Miss Bookmark replies,
"Without Book, I wouldn't have a place
to keep me safe.
The wind would just blow me away."

"Your pages are like cotton quilts, keeping me warm all the time. Thanks for your kindness friend." said Miss Bookmark.

Reader speaks up to Book,
"Do you feel that love?

You are a book.
You help teach kids how to read,
you make libraries cool,

and you even give short people a boost!

I think that's very kind of you and
not to mention you are super, duper funny!"

HARD BACK

STRONG
SPINE

Just think about it,
you have a hard back,
a strong spine,
and even a paper cover.

Book, you have a lot
to be thankful for.

PAPER COVER

You are a special book and quite honestly, I've never read one like you.

You are my favorite!

Book responds,
as the love and truth
touched every page of him,

"I am?"

Thank you Reader!

From this moment forward, I will be thankful for all the qualities that make me special. I will not let any other readers make me feel sad or alone anymore.

I AM A GREAT BOOK!

I AM SPECIAL!

Libraries, classrooms, English teachers, mothers, fathers, aunts, uncles, spider monkeys, caterpillars, choo choo trains, giraffes, hippos, dinosaurs,

one legged pirates, Santa Claus, Rudolph the red-nose reindeer,

gorillas,
  polar bears,
    coffee shops,
      toy stores,
        pizza palaces...

Here I come!

AUTHOR
IVON HICKMON

The youngest of three boys, son of Military Parents, Ivon found that his dreams of playing among the NFL greats were closer than he'd ever imagine. Ivon's football career journeyed from "last man" on the roster to earning his football scholarship with honors of being selected as Team Captain and MVP. Life threw test and trails at Ivon but somehow, he made it out. Ivon passionately serves Sport teams through his incredibly, inspiring, life changing experiences he conquered through many trail and errors.

A true "Girl Dad", Ivon spends hours a month visiting both his Daughter's school, cultivating young scholars through the power of reading. These visits propelled Ivon to release his debut Children's Book, "The Book Nobody Wanted to Read...Besides You", a fun & silly book that introduces kids to Emotional Intelligence & Inclusion. Ivon believes that the earlier kids can understand Emotional Intelligence, the more empowered they will become and the more that kids learn about inclusion, we will see unity.

Ivon is Husband to his Queen & College Sweetheart and Father of two Queens in training.

Ivon's mission is to Serve, Empower, and Connect with the Young Scholars, Student-Athletes, and Business Professionals whether it's through his inspirational speaking or through his book.

Made in the USA
Columbia, SC
13 June 2023

17841039R20020